Touched By

MESSAGES OF HOPE AND INSPIRATION FROM THE POPULAR TELEVISION PROGRAM

SAMPLE PAGE

You're not always going to hear the angels. When little children get older, other voices drown the angel voices out. But you should never stop listening for them. Sometimes you'll hear them in the trees. Sometimes you'll hear them in the crickets at dusk. Sometimes you'll only hear an angel in the sound of "hello." But never stop listening. And never forget that you did once hear them. And someday, you'll hear them again.

ISBN 1-58375-410-5

9 781583 754108

7 46962 00410 5

A DayBrightener™ product from

GARBORG'S
BLOOMINGTON, MINNESOTA

DS 18546

Through the mouths and the
hearts of children God
is speaking to you.

JULY 2

$\mathcal{E}$very person on this earth
is like a violin. Whatever wood
we're made of, whatever unique and
distinctive qualities we have, the
music is always the purest and the
most beautiful when we put
ourselves in the hands
of the Master.

JULY 1

God always has a plan, but He doesn't always hand it to us on a silver platter. Sometimes we have to learn the hard way.

— JULY 3

Tomorrow's a new day. Never forget to reach a bit further and take one more step. Follow your dreams wherever they lead.

JUNE 30

am a great and sublime fool,
but yet I am God's fool, and all
His works must be contemplated
with respect.

JULY 4

There's a rhythm to life. What
we do has eternal consequences,
and you've got to have faith that
whatever job you're given,
it matters.

JUNE 29

To whom much is given,

much is expected.

JULY 5

God lives in the praises
of His people.

JUNE 28

I am a soldier in God's army,
and there's no authority
higher than His.

JULY 6

*Y*ou're looking for clues about who you are. Find out who God is first because He made you.

JUNE 27

When you walk down the road,
heavy burden, heavy load, I will
rise and I will walk with you. When
you walk through the night, and
you feel like just giving up the
fight, I will comfort you, and you
will rise and I will walk with you.

JULY 7

Why would anyone rely on luck
when they have God's honest truth?
The truth that He loves them.

JUNE 26

Sweetheart, we're all on the same team, trying to win the game together. And don't you forget who's calling the plays for all of us.

JULY 8

God is faithful. He'll forgive
you even if you can't. His mercies
are brand new every morning.

JUNE 25

You'd be surprised how much baggage people carry around with them. Especially the kind you can't see. Half the time it's filled with the past. And looking inside can be the most important thing a person ever does.

JULY 9

Angels fail. Humans fail.

Only God does not fail.

JUNE 24

*D*on't be afraid. God loves you.
So much you can't even imagine it.

JULY 10

$\mathcal{L}$ook, I'll spell it out for you:
We mess up sometimes. You haven't
exactly thrown God for a loop,
you know. He can handle it.

JUNE 23

$\mathcal{G}$od can make the darkness go
away, and He will, in His own time.

Just trust Him.

JULY 11

*D*ear God, I want to thank You
for this day. This horrible, awful,
terrible day. Because if it wasn't for
You, I wouldn't have had any day
at all, so I thank You.

JUNE 22

$\mathcal{G}$od is here. The fastest car in the world can't outrun Him, and the toughest heart in the world can't ignore Him. Wherever you go, God will be there ahead of you, waiting for you with a miracle.

JULY 12

*Y*ou're on a great journey. One that will bring you much joy. Some sorrow, some frustration, maybe a headache, some lower back pains, but mostly joy.

JUNE 21

God's not just a matchmaker.

He's a matchkeeper.

JULY 13

Just because you're a person of faith doesn't mean you won't make mistakes. It means that when no one will understand why you made them, you know that God will. And it means that when no one can forgive you, you know that God can.

JUNE 20

Having seen God and His kingdom, angels already know what humans must simply have faith in. It is that quality of faith and the occasional doubts we must overcome that give humans a strength that angels can only admire.

JULY 14

$\mathcal{S}$ ometimes holding out a hand to
a stranger can be the hardest thing
in the world to do. But once you've
done it, you're not holding the
hand of a stranger any more.

JUNE 19

Father, here we are. We're
looking for truth. We're looking for
peace. We need Your mercy right
now, and we need Your wisdom.

JULY 15

"The quality of mercy is not strained...." Before Shakespeare said it, God was it. Mercy is His gift. You shine with His divine light every time you are merciful and forgive someone.

JUNE 18

The truth will always find a
way out. It can be hidden for years,
but it never gets lost, because the
truth comes from God.

JULY 16

God's love has no drought. He'll
water the garden of your soul
if you let Him.

JUNE 17

God has a mission for you.

JULY 17

*W*hen you take a step toward
God, He'll step toward you.

JUNE 16

*D*on't go questioning what God has for you to do. A famous man once said, if a man is called to be a street sweeper, he should sweep the streets so well that the angels will look down out of heaven and be proud.

JULY 18

Your life is a gift from God,
but He can't live it for you.

JUNE 15

You exchanged your faith for evidence. You stopped believing in what you knew, and you started believing in what you saw. But you see, faith is the evidence of what you can't see.

JULY 19

Everybody's faxing and modeming and onlining and inputting and downloading and overnighting. You can send anything to anybody, anywhere in the world in seconds. But it still takes the same time it always took to know a soul, to mend a broken heart...to give birth to a child. Even in a world of change, some things just don't.

JUNE 14

God doesn't need science to explain Himself.

JULY 20

In a world that demands
so much of you every minute
of every day, there is One who
knows who you really are
and loves you anyway.

JUNE 13

God can do anything and right now, He wants to save your life.

JULY 21

God can take anything that's broken and make it whole. But you must give Him the pieces. He's the Creator, and He can take all the pieces and make them fit together.

JUNE 12

The Almighty God sends angels
to this earth to bring messages,
to comfort, to provide protection
and deliver healing.

JULY 22

We have to fight evil–not
with our fists, but with
the power of God.

JUNE 11

There are some things that humans will find difficult to fully understand on this side of heaven, but I'm here to assure you that God is faithful and worthy of your praise.

JULY 23

You have dreams. Dreams that
you're afraid to dream, a life that
you're afraid to live, prayers that
you're afraid to pray. And it all
seems too late, but it's not. God
loves you and He will
give you hope.

JUNE 10

There is a time for everything.
There's a time to live. There's a
time to die. There's a time to be
busy, and there's a time to rest.

JULY 24

$\mathcal{I}$’ve been sent by God to help you through this. No wings. No halos. Just love. That's what you need. And that's what God gives.

~ JUNE 9

I suppose that if God sends an
angel to bring you peace, it's
because you're going to need it.

JULY 25

There are so many lessons we have to learn as we grow up, and sometimes we learn them on the first try. But most of the time we learn best by our mistakes.

JUNE 8

*P*eople like to think that bad things only happen to faceless strangers in newspapers, until it happens to them. That's why faith must be strong now, before we need it.

JULY 26

You were born to serve your Heavenly Father. He gave you brains, a heart, talent, imagination, passion, and emotion.

JUNE 7

We live in a world where accidents happen. Floods, earthquakes, droughts, deaths. Bad things occur every day, but that doesn't mean that God isn't good, because He is.

JULY 27

The whole world is full of
wholly unredeemable creatures.
Just the kind of creatures
God loves to save.

JUNE 6

*N*ever forget, when you have lost your faith, when God is no longer real to you, go back. Go back to the last place you saw Him. He will be waiting for you there.

JULY 28

I promise you, there's more to God's plan than you can see or feel right now. Pray to the One who knows all the answers.

JUNE 5

Answers from God aren't always easy to receive, but they're hard to mistake.

JULY 29

*N*o one dies without God's
knowledge or without getting the
chance to know Him.

JUNE 4

God loves you. And He knows
the secrets of your heart. But
you've let the past come between
you and God. Turn the past over to
Him. He is strong enough to take
it. Give Him your future, too. And
He'll make you strong enough
to face it.

JULY 30

No matter what you've done,
God loves you. He wants to take
away any hatred you feel for
yourself. He wants to help you
set things right.

JUNE 3

*E*ven if it doesn't make sense
at the time, God can turn
anything around.

JULY 31

*J*ust remember two things.
One, you are never alone, and
two, there's no such thing
as a free lunch.

~ JUNE 2

You know, it's a funny thing about being afraid. It has this way of getting in your face so that it's all that you can see. There's always another choice out there. But as long as you're afraid, you'll never be able to see it.

AUGUST 1

The one who controls the stars, is God, and He controls the sun and the moon and the heavens, but He doesn't control our lives and He doesn't control our hearts. They belong to us, and He will speak to them only if we ask Him, if we wait and watch and listen.

JUNE 1

*F*rightened people often
hide behind anger. They
need understanding.

AUGUST 2

$\mathcal{N}$othing, not death or life or war, not the past, the present, or the future, no one, no creature on this earth, can separate you from the love of God.

MAY 31

It's so easy to go from love to hate. But from hate back to love, that's the hard part.

AUGUST 3

There's gonna be good times.
There's gonna be bad times. The
good Lord can use you all the time.

MAY 30

You can't find life's full value until you hand it over to God and ask Him to redeem it, to trade it in for a new life—the person you were always meant to be. Do you think God draws borders in His love? Everyone is equal in His eyes.

AUGUST 4

He will send His angels
to watch over you.

MAY 29

Nothing can separate you from
the love of God.

AUGUST 5

*G*od gives everyone a purpose.

MAY 28

*Human love is very complicated,
but God's love is very simple.*

AUGUST 6

*W*here would this country be if people stopped dreaming of ways to make this a better place to live?

MAY 27

I know it's not easy, but it's simple. Forgive.

AUGUST 7

May the road rise before you...may your swing be straight...may the ball fly high and far...and may God Himself bring you home.

MAY 26

There are some good people
in the world, people who don't
have to blow their own horn
to hear the music.

AUGUST 8

$\mathcal{I}$ actually prayed and asked God
if just one day I could do
something to make a difference.
Well, you know what they say: Be
careful what you pray for.

MAY 25

$\mathcal{I}$'ve met a lot of men who don't believe in angels, but I never met a man who didn't want to.

AUGUST 9

You don't have to build
a building or publish a magazine to
make a difference in the world. God
can use you right now, where you
are, if you will let Him.

MAY 24

$\mathcal{G}$od is not dead. He doesn't die just because you say so. But a part of you dies every time you tell yourself that.

AUGUST 10

*G*od heals me with reassuring love. Overwhelming, overcoming, redeeming love.

MAY 23

You want a role model? Look a lot higher than some guy who can knock down a three pointer. Look up. Look all the way up.

AUGUST 11

God understands. He suffers the
pain of His children, but even in
pain there is growth.

MAY 22

Why is it that when folks look
at an old face they never see
the child inside?

AUGUST 12

God shows people the difference between right and wrong, and then He lets them make up their own minds, make their own decisions.

*G*od notices you. He even
counts your tears.

AUGUST 13

*S*ometimes you get so busy
looking for the little bug that you
don't see the storm clouds
gathering that could wipe out
the whole garden.

MAY 20

If you ever get lost, remember
this: Seek and ye shall find, but
you must search with
all your heart.

AUGUST 14

$\mathcal{L}$ife can be hard, and when it
gets hard you're going to forget
everything about it that's beautiful.
But if you trust God for a
breakthrough, everything will
be all right.

MAY 19

*N*o one is ever without an
angel when they need one most.

AUGUST 15

There is a difference between what your heart feels and what it knows. Your heart is for holding things: joy, love, pain. But looking to your heart for an answer instead of praying for one can get you into trouble. The answer to prayer comes from God and listening to Him will never trip you up.

MAY 18

I am here to remind you that
God loves you and that you
should never give up.

AUGUST 16

All God asks is that we do our
best. He knows what's
in your heart.

MAY 17

God doesn't make mistakes, even if the plan is not clear to humans or angels. He knows what He's doing; He's been doing this for years!

AUGUST 17

$\mathcal{G}$od doesn't want to take. He wants to give. But He can't give you anything 'til you learn to trust Him.

MAY 16

God is the maker of time and
His timing is perfect.

AUGUST 18

*G*od loves you. He wants to deal

with what you can do right now.

Because "now" is all

you can change.

MAY 15

*Y*ou can't change the world all at once. You've got to change it one life at a time.

AUGUST 19

$\mathcal{G}$od will lead you to fulfill
a wonderful purpose.

MAY 14

Sometimes it takes a lot of courage to keep a promise.

AUGUST 20

God isn't taking something away from you. He's giving you something. It's a gift. The chance to start over. God is there to mend your heart and heal your soul. But you have to let Him in.

MAY 13

God loves you...because you're you. You've spent your whole life running and running, trying to catch up with something that has never been there for you. And all you've done is go farther and farther away from the precious love that's been waiting for you all the time.

AUGUST 21

God wants you to cleanse your body and to cleanse your soul. He'll help you go through that cleansing if only you'll ask Him.

MAY 12

*D*on't be afraid. I'm an angel,
sent by God to tell you that fear
has no place in your life.

AUGUST 22

You can't undo anything you've already done, but you can face up to it. You can tell the truth. You can seek forgiveness. And then let God do the rest.

MAY 11

*I*f you can't find the love, let
God love through you.

AUGUST 23

*L*ove is never really lost. You
always find it again through God
because He loved you
first and best.

MAY 10

$\mathcal{P}$arents are a gift from God. But they are not a replacement for God. Because God will never die, He will never leave you. He is Life itself and He will never grow old.

AUGUST 24

Your body was created to be
the temple of something much more
precious than physical life. Your
body will die someday, somehow.
But your spirit, the true you—that
is where your real life is to be
found, and that is what God
wants to heal today.

MAY 9

God can't make mistakes or
change His mind. It's not
in His nature.

AUGUST 25

Mothers are one of God's greatest miracles.

MAY 8

God knows how lost you have felt, and He knows how alone you have been, but if you ask Him for direction right here, right now, He will put you on a new road. It may not be easy, but it will be a worthy journey that matters, and it will last for the rest of your life.

AUGUST 26

A tomato is very much like a
human soul. It takes a long time to
ripen, and it bruises real easy.

MAY 7

*I*t doesn't do you any good
to keep running, because you
can't run from God.

AUGUST 27

Humans make mistakes. They stumble, they lose their way, and so sometimes they need an angel.

MAY 6

*Y*ou've been playing hide-and-seek with your life. You cover your eyes thinking no one can see you, that no one will find you. Well, God never lost you.

AUGUST 28

*W*here there is faith,
it is never too late.

MAY 5

All your life you've been afraid
of life. You'd decide you were too
fat or too short or too anything,
as long as it could convince you
to hide. But God made you and
He knew what He was doing.

AUGUST 29

Babies are the evidence of
God's abiding love for man. That He
hasn't given up on the human race.

MAY 4

*H*ere's a tip from me to you:
don't blame God for what you don't
have. Thank Him for what
you do have.

AUGUST 30

*Y*our Father in heaven has
always loved you. He was very glad
that you were born and He's very
proud of you.

MAY 3

When you stand before God,
don't you want to see the face of
a friend instead of a stranger?

AUGUST 31

Father, please forgive us. We
are falling, lift us up. We are
frightened, comfort us with
Your peace. We are lost,
come and find us.

MAY 2

People have been painting pictures and writing songs and making movies about heaven ever since they could breathe, but they have never even come close.

SEPTEMBER 1

*L*et me help you understand something about God. What's good in the world, God made it. This would include babies, sunsets, and three-day weekends. The bad stuff in the world comes from somebody else entirely.

MAY 1

Love doesn't need a work permit.

SEPTEMBER 2

God doesn't leave us when we mess up. That's when we need Him most, and He'd never leave us when we need Him.

APRIL 30

We feel we have so much to lose in this world. But then you realize if God is there for you, there really isn't that much to lose.

SEPTEMBER 3

No one is ever really alone.

APRIL 29

*Y*ou should never be afraid
to tell the truth.

SEPTEMBER 4

*W*hat you're feeling is the

presence of God. He is here,

with us, right now.

APRIL 28

*D*eath.... It's probably one of the most real thing that happens on earth. It's awesome and profound, like a birth. The soul passing from one realm to another.

SEPTEMBER 5

God's hand holds us all up and
showers us with blessings.

APRIL 27

There but for the grace
of God go I.

SEPTEMBER 6

Real love, God's kind of love,
doesn't let you fall, it lifts you up.

APRIL 26

*H*as God ever forsaken you? He told you He wouldn't, and He never has. Never. Just because you feel invisible doesn't mean you are.

SEPTEMBER 7

God has not given you a spirit
of fear, but of power and of love.
And He has given you a sound
mind, a good mind.

APRIL 25

God doesn't cause pain. He heals it. He doesn't hate. He loves.

SEPTEMBER 8

You can do all things through
Him who gives you strength.

Just ask.

APRIL 24

People are always trying to build a stairway to heaven. But there's never been one that was high enough to make it all the way to God. That's when a soul has to stand on the top step and call up and say, "Here! Here I am. Please lift me up the rest of the way!" And God hears you. He reaches down and takes you home.

SEPTEMBER 9

Do you know why God put people's faces on the front of their bodies? Faces are in the front so people can see where they're going, not where they've been. We have to go forward, not backward.

APRIL 23

$\mathcal{G}$od is not taking anything
away from you. The world takes
things away from us. God restores
them, a thousand times better.

SEPTEMBER 10

God loves you and you don't
have to do anything to
deserve His love.

APRIL 22

Actually, God is not all that difficult to find.

SEPTEMBER 11

Who you are is not your name
or your family. Who you are is
more essential than that; it comes
from God. And what you make of
yourself, that is what you
give back to God.

APRIL 21

$\mathcal{G}$od wanted your heart to feel,
not hide. He never intended your
heart and your mind to be broken.
But they were, and you've locked
them away, and now you're afraid
if you open the door, you'll never
stop crying. But God made you
a person with tears, too.

SEPTEMBER 12

God wants every person to be
a whole person. A completely
unique individual, not half
of someone else.

APRIL 20

Even if you don't believe in God,

He believes in you.

SEPTEMBER 13

Even if every one of your good deeds was a step to heaven, it would never reach high enough. Only God's mercy can take you there.

APRIL 19

You can't change who you were.
But God will help you change who
you are. And today, you can
start over. Right now.

SEPTEMBER 14

You asked God for His help and
He's giving it to you. He has been
beside you through it all, and
He is with you now.

APRIL 18

*Nothing can sneak up on you
when you face it straight on.*

SEPTEMBER 15

*G*od chooses you to be His voice at this important time, and you can do it. Deliver His truth.

APRIL 17

You may feel alone, but you're not. God will not abandon you.

SEPTEMBER 16

There will be some difficult days, but your angels are here with you, and you will not be alone.

APRIL 16

The thing about the truth
is that it doesn't change and
it doesn't go away.

SEPTEMBER 17

Sometimes you have to stand up and fight for what you believe in. And sometimes it takes even more courage to stay put. To hold your ground and refuse to be bullied.... It doesn't change the bully. But it can change you.

APRIL 15

There is random violence in
this world because people have
a choice, but there are
no random angels.

SEPTEMBER 18

God puts into your spirit things
that could never come out
of your own mind.

APRIL 14

There's nothing to be afraid of.
On one side, there is life. And on
the other...there is life, too.

SEPTEMBER 19

*W*hatever you think you've
gotta win, He's already won for
you, if you'll just take hold of it.
That real prize is God and His love.
Set your eyes on that. That's the
only thing worth winning.

APRIL 13

I know that when you speak the truth and when you stop hiding and running, your heart and your mind will find peace.

SEPTEMBER 20

There are rewards out there waiting for you and bright skies and loving friends and a life so full you can't even begin to imagine. Oh, God loves you so much.

APRIL 12

*Every worthwhile search
starts with God.*

SEPTEMBER 21

God is not the source of
confusion. He is the source and
completer of your faith. And that is
what you need now. Faith that God
knows who you really are. Yes, you
are not perfect. No one is perfect.
No one. But God's love is perfect.
And no one can love us better
than He can.

APRIL 11

*T*he wonders of the universe,
the physics, the thermodynamics,
the medicines that are found in the
rain forest, the gene sequence in
a chromosome, those belong to God.

SEPTEMBER 22

God loves you. And if God is on your side, what is there to fear? Nothing. Now or ever.

APRIL 10

od loves you. He thinks
about you all the time.

SEPTEMBER 23

You don't have to be perfect
to receive God's love.

APRIL 9

A good relationship is supposed to add to your life, not take away from it. It should feel like a beautiful gift.

SEPTEMBER 24

*Y*ou've had setbacks, and you'll have others. It's not important how many times you've fallen. It's how many times you let God pick you up that matters.

APRIL 8

$\mathcal{I}$t's a dangerous thing to put people up on a pedestal. Humans have a way of slipping off and landing smack on their faces.

SEPTEMBER 25

*H*umbling yourself before your
Creator and asking for advice is a
sign of strength, not weakness.

APRIL 7

*Friends let friends
into their lives.*

SEPTEMBER 26

God has many names, you know. Jehovah, Almighty, Everlasting Father, Alpha and Omega.... But do you know what He calls Himself? "I Am." Ask God who He is and that is what He'll tell you. "I Am." Not "I was," or "I'm going to be." But "I Am." "I Am here for you now because that's where you need me." And if God is here, right here, right now, what is there to fear?

APRIL 6

Why did God create humanity?
He wanted to share His love.

SEPTEMBER 27

hy is it, if you talk to God,
you're praying, but if God talks to
you, you're nuts?

APRIL 5

*Y*ou don't have to be an angel.
You just have to believe. That's all
that God asks of you. He'll
take care of the rest.

SEPTEMBER 28

There is peace that you fight for with your soul. If you face the truth and fight the fight, then you will have a victory that may be called triumphant, and you will have peace that may be called lasting.

APRIL 4

God is not a hallucination. He's very real. He wants to help you.

SEPTEMBER 29

God wants you to let go of the
fear of being alone.

APRIL 3

God created you to be just who
you are. Nobody else can
be that. Only you.

SEPTEMBER 30

You're vulnerable, like everybody, to the things that weaken the soul—fear, prejudice, confusion. But you've got a good heart, and God can use that if you'll let Him.

APRIL 2

*G*od will never abandon you. He will never leave you or forsake you. That's the difference between God and people. People sometimes let you down, but God never will because He loves you perfectly, unconditionally.

OCTOBER 1

God loves you, and His love
is what gives you the strength to
go on to face your successes
and your failures.

APRIL 1

Choose to believe that God will never leave you or forsake you.

OCTOBER 2

It may be a long night, but the
morning will come, I promise you.
Just keep your eye on the
mountaintop. God's there
waiting for you.

MARCH 31

*Here we are, Lord. Show us
the way to carry on.*

OCTOBER 3

*G*od will give you the strength.
His hand is right in front of you.
All you have to do is reach out
and take it.

MARCH 30

*G*od wants you to choose life.
No one else can do that for you,
not even God Himself.

OCTOBER 4

$\mathscr{G}$od has a plan for your life.

There is a reason for you

to be living.

MARCH 29

It takes time to master the art of watching and waiting. Some of the wisest minds in history didn't get it down, but it's important.

OCTOBER 5

Because God loves us so much,
He gives us freedom.

MARCH 28

Fear is a thief. It will steal all your todays by making you dread tomorrow.

OCTOBER 6

$\mathcal{G}$od isn't magic. And neither is the Bible. Quoting it isn't enough. You've got to live it. From inside. That's where the changes take place, inside you.

MARCH 27

People laugh at God, they take His name in vain, they say He's dead, they ignore Him completely, and it happens every day. You don't see Him give up, and He wants you to learn how to hang in there, too.

OCTOBER 7

God would never turn

His back on you.

MARCH 26

It's not something in your genes, like your mother's eyes or your grandmother's nose. No, faith is something you've got to work out for yourself. And it doesn't happen in the good times. Your parents forged their faith, one failure at a time.

OCTOBER 8

Chance disappears when you
make a decision.

MARCH 25

Nothing's more dangerous than loving. Unless it's not loving. Look, He's not promising that it's going to be easy, but He says it's going to be worth it.

OCTOBER 9

*J*ust keep your heart and your
eyes open and God will show you
exactly what to do.

MARCH 24

Will you wake up and stop just smelling the coffee? Sooner or later, you gotta drink it. It's like life. You never really know how good it is until you taste it.

OCTOBER 10

There are people to cherish and hearts to change. There is a life to live here. And He will hold your hand all the way if you will just come into the light and have faith.

MARCH 23

*G*od offers you a choice.
Forgiveness and peace or separation
from Him, forever.

OCTOBER 11

God wants to help you, if
you'll let Him.

MARCH 22

$\mathscr{D}$on't you understand that
winning a lottery is not a miracle?
Stop looking outside of
yourself for answers.

OCTOBER 12

Isn't it odd that people pray every day over the tiniest things–the weather, a green light, a baseball game, things they can't change at all. But why do people forget to pray when they are faced with a big decision? When there's a difficult choice to make, don't you think God would like to help you make it?

MARCH 21

$\mathcal{N}$othing is impossible.

OCTOBER 13

$\mathscr{G}$od always listens. I have that
on high authority. I promise you.

MARCH 20

When children stop asking
questions, that's when
we've got problems.

OCTOBER 14

$\mathcal{I}$f you're searching for
something in your life, seek God
first, and then He will make sure
you have everything else
that you need.

MARCH 19

The love has always been there
for you. All you needed was the
courage to hold on to it.

OCTOBER 15

$\mathcal{G}$od loves you. He will not fail you. He wants you to know that He will walk with you all the way, but it's up to you to take the first step.

MARCH 18

*Y*ou know that God has not left you alone in this. He does not want you to judge yourself or anyone else. He wants you to do what you've always done: be His child and let Him comfort you. Nobody can do that better than He can right now.

OCTOBER 16

*D*on't put your complete trust
in the work of your own hands.

MARCH 17

$\mathcal{G}$od turns everything around,
all the time, so something good's
got to come out of this.... I just
can't tell you when. And remember,
He'll never leave or forsake you.

OCTOBER 17

Every day is a chance to start over, my friend.

MARCH 16

Have you ever noticed how even people who don't believe in God find themselves calling out His name in their lowest, loneliest hour? You can't ask for His help unless somewhere, deep down, you truly believe in Him.

OCTOBER 18

When we've lost hope, when our hearts are hard and hopeless, God can soften them and fill them with hope once again. He is able to do that. But you have to ask Him to. Right now. This is your chance to start the miracle.

MARCH 15

It's hard sometimes. Knowing
the what, but not always
knowing the why.

OCTOBER 19

There are two kinds of people in this world–the one's who tear down and the ones who build up.

MARCH 14

God is able to heal anything and anyone. He made your body and He can heal your body of any disease. But your body was created to be the temple of something much more precious than physical life. Your spirit, the true you–that is where your real life is to be found, and that is what God wants to heal today.

OCTOBER 20

*G*od will always answer when
you seek His counsel.

MARCH 13

God loves you and He wants to give you a new name—a name that means victory. True victory, the kind that wins at the game of life.

OCTOBER 21

The "what ifs" and the "if onlys" will only make it harder to heal. Don't ask those questions.

MARCH 12

If a person walks away from
God, where else is there to go?

OCTOBER 22

God loves all of His creations.
And that includes you, and
that includes me.

MARCH 11

*A*nyone can give up, it's the easiest thing in the world to do. But to hold it together when everyone would understand if you fell apart, that's true strength.

OCTOBER 23

You've got the most powerful
weapon of all. Love. Stick to it.
Evil can't stay around
where there is love.

MARCH 10

$\mathcal{G}$od didn't set this journey in motion. He's just as angry as you are that you have to walk this road. But He promises you this, He will walk this road with you. And He will be there for you when you reach the end of it. God loves you.

OCTOBER 24

God doesn't give you what you deserve. He gives you what He wants you to have: The best of everything, because He loves you. All you have to do is ask.

MARCH 9

How can you judge something fairly when you don't know what the rules are? You can't play God because you aren't God.

OCTOBER 25

Don't look for the faith to believe...leap for it. For a second there you're not hanging onto anything and it's very scary, but that's just when God lifts you up.

MARCH 8

It's time to turn judgment into
compassion. Pain into healing.
Hate into forgiveness.

OCTOBER 26

The gift of God's love. It's a
miracle you can give to everyone.

MARCH 7

*H*ell is separation from God.
It's an eternity without light. If
you were on your way there, God
wasn't sending you. You were
sending yourself.

OCTOBER 27

God never said, "Make
a beautiful noise unto the Lord."
He said, "Make a joyful noise."

MARCH 6

When two people are on
a journey, there will be miles when
they will fall silent, but that
doesn't mean they shouldn't
be traveling together.

OCTOBER 28

Without forgiveness there
is no healing.

MARCH 5

When people look the other way they can lose a french fry, or they can lose something a lot more precious. Maybe even their soul.

Father, help us to face the
challenges of our lives. Help us to
love each other. Help us to open
our hearts even unto strangers.

MARCH 4

You've always been a child of God, and that should have been enough. But you wanted more. And at what price? What is it going to matter if you gain the whole world and lose your soul?

OCTOBER 30

*G*od's got a plan. It's like the
wind; just because you can't see it
doesn't mean it's not there.

MARCH 3

*The miracle is that there isn't
more evil in this world
than there is.*

OCTOBER 31

*A*ngels don't make everything
okay. We just introduce you
to the One who can.

MARCH 2

*I*t is not faith in your fathers that survives from generation to generation. It is the faith of your fathers. It lives here, now, and it is yours to grasp. It is the real help in times of trouble. It is the legacy your fathers have left and the gift God has given you.

NOVEMBER 1

When we share our dreams with God, He won't laugh. As a matter of fact, God will take our dreams more seriously than we do, because He knows no compromise. He doesn't deal in pieces of happiness and shadows of dreams. He will ask more of us than we ask of ourselves, but He will return more to us than we could ever hope or imagine ourselves.

MARCH 1

You're not always going to hear
the angels. But you should never
stop listening for them.

NOVEMBER 2

There is someone who wants to
see you finish what you began,
with the best that you have–God.

FEBRUARY 29

*W*e've got to teach children
that life is the most precious
thing they have.

NOVEMBER 3

We're not here to make it easier. We're here to make it better.

FEBRUARY 28

The truth is sometimes hard to face, but when you do, you will rise above it and be freed.

NOVEMBER 4

There are rivers for you to cross, but when you walk through the waters, God will be with you. There are mountains for you to climb. But when you cannot take another step...He will carry you.

FEBRUARY 27

My choice of coffee is a good ol' cup of joe. Straight ahead. Honest. No camouflage... 'cause when you try to hide what's underneath, you just end up feeling miserable.

NOVEMBER 5

Shame brings you down. But true humility will only lift you higher.

FEBRUARY 26

There have been times when
you've been so afraid about letting
God down that you forgot
about His mercy.

NOVEMBER 6

When you put other people
before yourself, that shows you
know God and who He is.

FEBRUARY 25

If God is willing to forgive you, who are you not to forgive yourself? You think you know better than God?

NOVEMBER 7

All I want to do is count
my blessings. To be grateful in
the little moments in life.

FEBRUARY 24

Only God has the right to take a life or give one back. Let Him give yours back to you. Let Him help you find mercy for those who fail.

NOVEMBER 8

Forgiveness is such a powerful
thing, and your act of forgiveness
can be someone's answer to prayer.

FEBRUARY 23

$\mathcal{I}$ don't know what others will say when they hear the truth, but I know that when you speak it and when you stop hiding and running, your heart and your mind will find peace.

NOVEMBER 9

God gives you everything that
you need to fulfill your own unique
purpose in this world.

FEBRUARY 22

Every child is a miracle.

NOVEMBER 10

*S*omeone once told me that it
has to get really dark before
you can see the stars.

FEBRUARY 21

God always sends His angels
wherever they are needed.

NOVEMBER 11

*Hiding a problem doesn't make
it go away. As a matter of fact,
keeping an ugly problem
in the dark just makes
it bigger and uglier.*

FEBRUARY 20

You know, we forget that love
is a choice, and we have to make
that choice every day.

NOVEMBER 12

Remember who you are.

A child of God.

FEBRUARY 19

$\mathcal{I}$ don't know where. And I don't know when. The only thing I do know is that the kind of love worth waiting for, you won't have to lie for, or steal, or keep hidden in a box to visit on weekends.

NOVEMBER 13

*D*ear God, sometimes You speak
in a whisper. Sometimes You shout
into our lives. But Your word
is always true.

FEBRUARY 18

*Evil thrives when good men
do nothing.*

NOVEMBER 14

$\mathcal{G}$od's mercy lasts a lot longer
than any trouble you'll ever
find yourself in.

FEBRUARY 17

$\mathcal{W}$hy do you care about being
loved for your success when you're
already loved as a person and
a child of God?

NOVEMBER 15

You've been looking for reasons instead of peace. And there will never be enough reasons. But God will always give you enough peace.

FEBRUARY 16

When we ignore the truth, we ignore God, because God is truth.

NOVEMBER 16

God, sometimes I take You for granted. All this work, all the lists, what's it all for without You right in the middle of it? So, Lord, bless this day.

FEBRUARY 15

$\mathcal{G}$ive some people a glimpse of heaven and they're off and singing. But some people, you can put heaven right smack in front of 'em, and they still can't see anything to sing about.

NOVEMBER 17

God has a message for you. He wants you to know that He loves you, that only He can fill that emptiness inside. You just have to open your heart to His truth.

FEBRUARY 14

You've got to start worshiping
something higher than yourself,
man, 'cause I've got news for you:
you are nowhere near as cool
as God is.

NOVEMBER 18

*Funny, isn't it, how you have
to be silent sometimes before
you can communicate.*

FEBRUARY 13

*D*o you really think that
you have the power to
mess up God's plans?

NOVEMBER 19

God always gives you what you

need when you need it.

FEBRUARY 12

*O*nly you are responsible for

your faith in God.

NOVEMBER 20

$\mathcal{L}$earning how to forgive, that's really tough. It's easier to stay mad. But unless we learn how to really forgive, we never learn how to really love.

FEBRUARY 11

*W*hy do people care about magic when God creates miracles?

NOVEMBER 21

Angels aren't fairies flapping
their wings and granting wishes.
Angels are messengers of God,
not ends in themselves.

FEBRUARY 10

Train up a child in the way he should go, and when he is old he will not depart from it. God said it and it will happen. Whether you're there to see it or not.

NOVEMBER 22

$\mathcal{T}$imes change, people change, interest rates change, even the land itself can change. But God is the same yesterday, today and forever.

FEBRUARY 9

There is no greater love than
to give your life for a friend.

NOVEMBER 23

You see, faith is the evidence of what you can't see.

FEBRUARY 8

*I*t takes a lot of faith for people to hear God.

NOVEMBER 24

No one really knows you or understands you completely except the One who made you.

FEBRUARY 7

Father in heaven, we are so
grateful for the bounty we see
before us. And for all the
wonderful things that have come to
us from Your hands. We're
especially grateful for each other.

NOVEMBER 25

Why is it no one pays
attention to the light until it
disappears into the darkness?

*T*hank you, Lord, for this Thanksgiving meal, and thank You for the hands that prepared it. Thank You for all the gifts we take for granted every day. Thank You for always remembering the big things, like oxygen and the sun coming up every day, and the little things, like cranberry sauce and fiber optics. Thank You especially for bringing us all here together today.

NOVEMBER 26

There are honest people in this
world. People who deserve to be
your heroes. And guess what? God
can even make a hero out of you
if you let Him.

FEBRUARY 5

This is what you call an unexpected snow. One moment the sky looks clear and the next moment, the sky is falling. And you can run inside and hide, or you can become part of it and let it change you.

NOVEMBER 27

Angels don't bring confusion.

They bring truth.

FEBRUARY 4

God watches over every soul.

NOVEMBER 28

God doesn't care how smart you
are. He cares about what's
in your heart.

FEBRUARY 3

Forgiveness won't change the other person. It will change you.

NOVEMBER 29

$\mathcal{G}$od is faithful. He will stick with you even when you won't. He will forgive you even when you can't. His mercies are brand new every morning.

FEBRUARY 2

Why would God send an angel to me?... Just to let you know that there's somebody who's never going to leave you. That He's going to love you always. That's His promise.

NOVEMBER 30

This morning, He wants to give
this day to you, and all the rest
of your days, too. All you have
to do...is say "yes."

FEBRUARY 1

You never know when you're
entertaining an angel.

DECEMBER 1

*E*very person must make a
choice about whether to spend their
life standing in the darkness and
worrying or stepping over into the
light and living to the fullest.

JANUARY 31

There is mercy for you in
heaven, even though it's hard
to find on earth.

DECEMBER 2

With God there is no time. Yesterday, today, and tomorrow all belong to Him, right now. And He's willing to give it all to you, this instant, if you'll accept it.

JANUARY 30

God will never leave us nor
forsake us. Not now or ever.

DECEMBER 3

Truth penetrates your heart in a way that mere words cannot.

JANUARY 29

What we do in love
is never lost.

DECEMBER 4

*L*ots of people believe. But
trusting Him...that is
the next step.

JANUARY 28

*A*ngels do not allow themselves to be the focus of worship. Their purpose is to serve and glorify their Creator.

DECEMBER 5

God's not a stranger. He's the best friend you've got.

JANUARY 27

If you want the truth,
go to the Source.

DECEMBER 6

$\mathcal{D}$on't worry. It always works
out sooner or later. Cast your cares
on God, because He cares for you.

JANUARY 26

You don't have to change
your life. Just let God
change your heart.

DECEMBER 7

Faith doesn't get you around trouble, it gets you through it.

JANUARY 25

You've got to stop looking at yourself through your eyes and see yourself through God's eyes.

DECEMBER 8

$\mathcal{L}$ove doesn't hide. It stays and
fights. It goes the distance. That's
why God made love so strong. So it
can carry you...all the way home.

JANUARY 24

$\mathcal{G}$od sometimes gives us what
we need, not what we want.

DECEMBER 9

There is no reason to worry
about tomorrow. God is
already there.

JANUARY 23

God doesn't do things half way.
He doesn't give you some of His
love, He gives you all of His love.
He doesn't let you glimpse
just a part of your dream,
He lets you see it all.

DECEMBER 10

$\mathcal{Y}$ou always get through, always.
Sometimes you come through the
darkness back into the sunlight,
and sometimes you come through
into light itself. But whatever you
do, keep your eyes on the light.

JANUARY 22

People don't always have to be busy. Sometimes they should just sit back and enjoy the peace.

DECEMBER 11

Hearts can change in an instant, but they must be given the chance.

JANUARY 21

*S*ometimes it's our belief in God
and our acts of forgiveness, so
much like God's own, that show
others the way back home.

DECEMBER 12

*G*od may move in mysterious
ways. But people...their ways are
the biggest mystery of all.

JANUARY 20

*S*ometimes people just do things
for other people because it's the
nice thing to do.

DECEMBER 13

Free will is a gift.

Love is a choice.

But hate leaves you

no choice at all.

JANUARY 19

God gives us time to share
together, to become the friends we
were meant to be.

DECEMBER 14

There's only one thing in this world that is truly bulletproof. It's faith. The faith you wrap yourself up in every day of your life. Faith that no matter what happens, you won't lose God's love. And all the bullets in the world can't pierce it.

JANUARY 18

*W*hen you stop trying to create
your own sense of peace, God will
give you peace like this world
has never known.

DECEMBER 15

*M*an gives information.

God gives inspiration.

JANUARY 17

You're wrapped up in God's
love, no matter what happens today,
tomorrow, or ever.

December 16

"*No*" can be one of the most positive words in the world. "No, I have not surrendered. No, I will not give up."

JANUARY 16

There is love. Share it with everyone who walks through your door.

DECEMBER 17

$\mathcal{I}$ am an angel sent by God to tell you that He's here. He's always been here, and He wonders why you turn away from Him at the times you need Him most.

JANUARY 15

*A*ngels bring messages. They bring comfort. They can bring protection. They don't heal, but they can bring healing from God.

DECEMBER 18

Sometimes the act of forgiving
is not something you do for
another person, but something
you do for yourself.

JANUARY 14

God is watching us, and He sends His angels down to protect us and to advise us.

DECEMBER 19

How do you pray? Just tell God
what's in your heart.

JANUARY 13

God wants to bring you peace.

DECEMBER 20

$\mathscr{T}$rust Him with all those things that frighten you and all those things that hurt you. Trust Him with your hopes and your dreams. He just wants to be the best friend you've ever had.

JANUARY 12

*G*od's gift to you and to everyone at Christmas is: Fear not. Live in peace.

DECEMBER 21

You're one of God's creations
and He loves you.

JANUARY 11

*Remember, Christmas is
a time for miracles.*

DECEMBER 22

*D*ream as big as you can. But
hand those dreams over to God
who really cares about
what happens to you.

JANUARY 10

*C*hristmas comes no matter
what we do. Christmas, the birth
of hope, of a new spirit,
will always come.

DECEMBER 23

*L*ove is always a good choice.

JANUARY 9

And lo, there were in the same country shepherds keeping watch over their flocks by night. And behold, an angel of the Lord stood by them, and the brightness of God showed round about them, and they were greatly afraid, and the angel said unto them. "Fear not, for I bring you good tidings of great joy that shall be unto all people."

DECEMBER 24

The world is changed one
miracle at a time.

JANUARY 8

Hallelujah! For the Lord God Omnipotent reigneth.

DECEMBER 25

*W*ords of hope. Words that
give life. Words that sustain life.
Sometimes that's all
we have to give.

JANUARY 7

$\mathcal{W}$e have been given
a marvelous gift. A mystery has
occurred in our midst. A holy
visitation. We must not greet it
with panic and superstition. We
must cherish it, and hold it in our
hearts until we have learned what
God intends for us to do with it.

DECEMBER 26

God sends angels for many reasons. Sometimes, it is to help with death. Sometimes it's to help with life.

JANUARY 6

The only way to share a
friend's pain is to share their pain.

DECEMBER 27

No mistake you may have
ever made is bigger than
God's power to fix it.

JANUARY 5

God could change history every day. But then there would be no real freedom in the world.

DECEMBER 28

God creates us all in His image.
There are no second-class citizens,
no minorities, no human beings
greater or lesser than any other.
We are all the same in His eyes.

JANUARY 4

You're having the wrong kind of dreams, man. You can't waste your time dreaming about the past. You gotta stick to dreamin' about the future.

DECEMBER 29

When you cry, God cries with you. But He can only wipe your tears if you let Him.

Sometimes endings are
just opportunities.

DECEMBER 30

What you need to know about the past is that no matter what has happened, it has all worked together to bring you to this very moment. And this is the moment you can choose to make everything new. Right now.

JANUARY 2

This life is a flicker. It burns
white hot for an instant, and then
it's gone. But it sets the course for
the eternity to come.

DECEMBER 31

*G*od sees you just exactly as
you are. He sees you more perfectly
and more truly than people can.
And He loves you more than
you can ever imagine.

JANUARY 1

Touched By An Angel

Design by Franke Design

Published by Garborg's, Inc.
P. O. Box 20132
Bloomington, MN 55420

ISBN 1-58375-410-5

Touched By An
ANGEL